MARTHA GALLARDO ESPINDOLA

Voices of the Soul

Primix Publishing
East Brunswick Office Evolution
1 Tower Center Boulevard, Ste 1510
East Brunswick, NJ 08816
www.primixpublishing.com
Phone: 1-800-538-5788

Published by Primix Publishing: 12/03/2024

ISBN: 979-8-89194-365-0(sc)
ISBN: 979-8-89194-366-7(e)

Library of Congress Control Number: 2024922083

CONTENTS

VOICE OF LOVE

VOICE OF SELF-DISCOVERY

VOICE OF WISDOM

VOICE OF LIGHT AND HOPE

VOICE OF LOVE

THE PRICE OF LOVE

If knowing you demands a fee,
I'll pay what love deems fair.
Among loves never meant to be,
I've tasted bitter air.

I thank not for this wounded heart,
But for the gift of you.
True love, a pain from heavens' art,
Brings sorrow, pure and true.

Why must I pay to see your eyes,
Or touch your silken hair?
I'll never let your memory die,
A stolen kiss I'll dare.

If for this theft I must atone,
I'll meet the price, I swear.
Ask not that I forget you, no—
Such pleas I cannot bear.

Even if heaven should demand,
I'd choose you, come what may.
From first sight, love took command,
Its cost I'll gladly pay.

For you, my dear, I'd pay any sum,
If fair for love, it's done.
No price too high, no cost too numb,
For you're my chosen one.

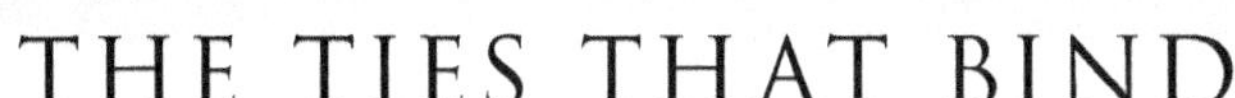

THE TIES THAT BIND

Rosa and María, reunited after years,
Found no joy in meeting, only haunting fears.
Memories weighed heavy on their hearts,
Of a childhood torn cruelly apart.

A mother's discontent, a father's neglect,
Left scars deeper than they could expect.
Among their siblings, they bore the most pain,
Their bond forged in sorrow, like links in a chain.

Rosa's words echo from that fateful day,
By the old tree where shadows hold sway:
"What sin bound us both to that spot?
Thunder crashed, lightning struck—we were distraught!"

Time crawled by, each moment an age,
As rain-soaked sisters trembled in rage.
Then Uncle Juan, a beacon in the storm,
Found them tied, shivering, forlorn.

"Good Lord, children! Who's done this to you?"
Their chattering teeth barely let words through.
With kindness, he freed them from their plight,
Wrapped them in blankets, held them tight.

Oh, the weight of those memories dire!
A childhood consumed by misfortune's fire.
Rosa, now gone, her struggles ceased,
Of María's fate, the world knows least.

Two sisters, bound by shared despair,
Now separated by time and air.
Their story lingers, a somber refrain,
Of ties that bind and enduring pain.

THE SPELL OF LOVE

Ensnared by your love, I stand enthralled,
Oh, beating heart of my very soul.
Moments with you I long to recall,
Each thrill is infinite, beyond control.

Though fleeting was our time entwined,
Our passion burned with fervent heat.
Days into weeks, so swift they climbed,
A month passed by, oh so sweet.

Yet think not that I'd die to see your face,
For if such love should lead to death's embrace,
I'd break the spell your fiery glances cast,

Returning the potion your lips did pour.
This enchantment, though sweet, cannot last,
Lest it consume me forevermore.

A THIEF'S KISS

Kiss me! My lips yearn for your tender touch,
Parched with love's thirst, they cry out at your sight.
One kiss from you would mean so much,
To quench this longing, set my world alight.

Kiss me with fire, with passion's fierce embrace,
With sweetness that could melt the hardest heart.
Let ardor burn across each inch of space
Between us, 'til we can no longer part.

Be bold, my love, and steal what I freely give,
This kiss I offer, silent in my plea.
Like a thief who knows love's fugitive
Delight, take what was always yours to seize.

And when at last our lips have met,
When thirst is quenched and passion spent,
Before you go, lest you forget,
I'll whisper words of love's intent:

"My darling, know this truth above all else:
My heart is yours, in love with you it dwells."

THE HEART'S QUANDARY

Verses flow from restless pen,
As slumber gently calls.
My thoughts, a maze without an end:
Whose love should catch my fall?

Carlos, he who gives me life,
A breath of sweet delight.
Juan, the source of tender strife,
A distant, longed-for sight.

Andrés, with ways that vex my soul,
Yet draws me ever near.
Three paths, each with a different toll,
Which one should I hold dear?

Juan, virtuous in my eyes,
A paragon of grace.
Yet distance between us lies,
A void I can't embrace.

In sleepless nights, I ponder still,
This choice that weighs so heavy.
For matters of the heart fulfill,
Yet leave the mind unsteady.

To whom should I my love bestow?
The answer still eludes.
For each holds sway, this much I know,
In different magnitudes.

LOVE'S WILLING SACRIFICE

I'll lay bare my heart, a pulsing truth,
And whisper words I've longed to say:
I love you beyond the dreams of youth,
With passion time cannot decay.

Though fear may tremble in my breast,
I'll not deny what's burning bright.
My heart, once guarded, now confessed,
Surrenders to love's sweet might.

Steal me with kisses, deep and true,
Let your gaze caress my soul.
I care not if the dawn breaks through,
For in your arms, I'm whole.

If your kiss brings heavenly bliss,
If your gaze should strike me dead,
Then let me fall to love's abyss—
I'll wear death's crown upon my head.

For in this love, I'm crucified,
A willing martyr to desire.
My heart and soul open wide,
Consumed by love's eternal fire.

VERSES OF THE HEART

Vivid author of my story's page,
Every poem born today bears your name.
Robber of my nights, you set the stage,
Stirring inspiration's endless flame.

Enlightened by your presence, I yearn
Secretly to steal a kiss so sweet.
Yet though I can't, let this truth be learned:
From first sight, my heart found its beat.

Silence your memory? I've tried in vain,
Escape your thoughts? An impossible feat.
Somehow you've become my joyous pain,
Etched within, making my soul complete.

Softly, I've caressed your flowing hair,
Skin beneath my touch, a silk delight.
You've awakened feelings beyond compare,
Emotions soaring to dizzying height.

Stay with me, my muse, my heart's desire,
For losing you would dim life's brightest star.
Each verse I write fuels love's growing fire,
Securing you near, both close and far.

A LOVE UNSPOKEN

If I could pen the words tucked in my heart,
My verses would reveal love's sweet art.

An enchanted smile that lifts my spirit's grace,
Wrapped in your caring gaze, your lovely face.

The sighs you steal and kisses oh so dear,
Imbued with passion that knows not fear.

Unspoken moments lost to yesteryear,
Embraces dreamed but never held so near.

Serenades imagined in the night's embrace,
Goodbyes delayed for your tender grace.

Thoughts left unsaid yet longing to confess,
Break on my lips that yearn to caress.

Still I wait to lay my soul bare to thee,
And pour my love in verse for you to see.

ON LOVE AND DESIRE

'Tis said that love and lust walk not the same,
One seeks surface, one runs soul deep and plain.

To dwell alone with you beneath the starlit sky,
The moon our lamp, the heavens our ceiling high.

To love as vast as ocean's swirling blue,
Watch winged ones soar as two hearts entwine anew.

Let hours flee and night its silken cloak unfold,
Screen us from day's toils in nature's embrace so bold.

Among rose bowers through mystic woodlands roam,
Repeating the bard's proverb—life itself is love's poem.

THE NATURE OF LOVE

Love is a breeze that blows through the soul,
A fleeting feel that comes, and takes its toll.

It dances upon the wind and lights the eye,
It wanders dreams by day, in slumbered sigh.

It bridges leagues that keep two hearts apart,
It feels the kiss that melts the inmost heart.

It knows the joy that washes guilt away,
When for love's sake one's guard does disobey.

FOR A GLIMPSE OF THEE

Within thine eyes I've seen heaven's twin gleams,
In thy sweet song, an angel's purest themes.

For one look from thee, I'd offer all I hold,
A verse and bloom, my worth but meager and cold.

Thy gazes flare through me like bolts of brand,
Wring sighs from my soul at thy slenderest command.
E'en should they end me I pray to see thee once more,
Fulfill this wretch's longing, his rapture restore.

Though denied thy presence, by God's will made so,
Still thee in my heart I evermore bestow.
Thy memory there enshrined shall never decay -
Thou'rt with me always, come what fateful day.

OUR LOVE'S HARMONY

Oh, to behold your face once more, my love,
And hold you near where our two hearts may rove.

To brush soft kisses on your cheek aglow,
My lips athirst your sweetness to know.

Within your eyes like oceans deep to drown,
Steal your sweet breath in bonds of love fast bound.

Twine close as stars that grace the celestial span,
As into your embrace my soul takes wing and fans

Dream's painted visions - moonlit bowers flowering,
Dragons azure whose breath mingles souls adoring.

Our loves find concord where none else may ken,
As lips to loving lips draw near again.

LONGING TO SEE YOU AGAIN

Here by my pillow lies your dear memory,
Sweetest face, yet brings sorrow's melody.

Your image from my heart refuses flight,
In soul's depths still you shed your light.

What shall I do with this love that burns so bright?
My joy turned gloom; my moon eclipsed by night.

To lose myself within your tender gaze,
Thither thoughts fly on love-winged ways.

Ah, but distance pains, how I ache to hold
Within these arms your warmth enfold.

Your voice's song entrances my yearning ear,
Who broke this heart now shed on parting tear?

Let me behold your beauty one time more,
Engrave your likeness on memory's shore,
Lest you fade and I forget you nevermore.

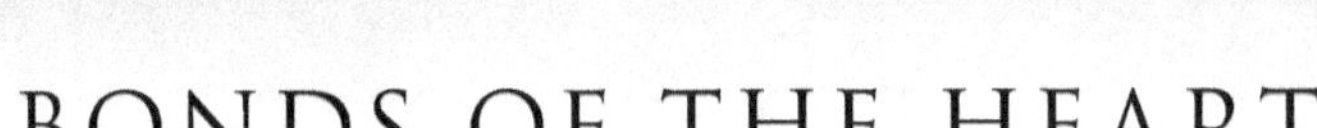

BONDS OF THE HEART

Come walk with easy step and linger nigh,
Let fond eyes trace thy lovely form and sigh.

Thy kindness bids dead feelings wake anew,
Thy wiles revive what sleeps no more in view.

Thy nightly presence at my side gives cheer,
In dreams enfolding souls that hold dear.

As shepherd tends his sheep at close o' dawn,
The bee its blossoms, farmer crops new born,

So shines thy grace that binds my heart through all,
In love's embrace finds harbor from life's thrall.

HIDDEN LOVE

A love concealed, a secret heart's desire,
A fleeting encounter, yet profound and true.
Though hidden deep, it sets my soul afire,
A phantom love I cannot yet pursue.

Though leagues may part us, still I feel him near,
His presence lingers, ghostlike in my mind.
Yet pride's high walls, they made him disappear,
Leaving only longing left behind.

The weight of absence pressed upon my frame,
I shed both tears and substance in my grief.
To heaven's ears, I whispered his dear name,
Imploring God to grant my heart relief.

As months unspooled their slow and measured tread,
I found a fragile solace in my pain.
In memories of one whose path had led
Away from mine, not to return again.

Yet time, that great physician of the soul,
Brought not forgetfulness, but something more.
That shadow from my past began to stroll
Once more across my heart's receptive floor.

It beckoned softly, asking for a place
To nest and grow, to blossom and take root.
With hesitance, I offered my embrace,
To nurture love from this unripened fruit.

Like wounded bird, it settled in my breast,
Its gentle presence slowly winning me.
Though out of sight, it would not let me rest,
A hidden love I could not help but see.

Though still concealed from every other eye,
I hold a faith that burns both strong and bright:
One day he'll come, beneath love's open sky,
To stay beside me in the clear daylight.

No more to stray, no more to hide away,
Our hidden love will finally see the day.

ICE AND YOU

What love is this—
A digital façade, a screen's cold glow?
Do you fathom the message
Your actions silently show?

You whisper of secrets untold,
Or perhaps it's courage you lack.
This is a love of ice,
As frigid as your heart's track.

Is your soul locked in winter,
Needing time to thaw and bloom?
Tell me, what shadows do you harbor,
What fears consume?

While you linger in darkness,
I'm left to guess and doubt.
If you need time to heal old wounds,
For heaven's sake, speak out!

But know this, my distant dear:
Your silence builds a wall.
And through this barricade of frost,
You'll never reach my heart at all.

HOW DO YOU WANT
ME TO LOVE YOU?

Your heart holds love, yet speak its truths with care
Desiring closeness, still your partner's freewill honor
With trust and understanding build your bond each day
Lest jealousy or control push love away

Torment not with accusations or mistrust
Nor point in blame when fears obscure your light
Open in empathy, in patience seek to understand
And heal in kindness any hurts on either side

True love respects each soul's autonomy
It dwells not in regrets but in present choice
With faith in their good heart, of deceit be not afraid
Upon free will is built intimacy unafraid

Force not your love where it is not felt
Coercion kills what care alone can grow
Nurture trust through equals' respect
And in your love find freedom, give freedom in its turn

FATAL ATTRACTION

You draw me in, a force magnetic,
Alluring, dangerous, hypnotic.
This pull, so potent it could kill,
Like venom coursing through my will.

A dagger plunged in beating heart,
Each pulse a surge of passion's art.
The wound, far from a mortal call,
Ignites desire's fiercest thrall.

Reason fades, a distant shore,
As thoughts of you flood evermore.
Obsession blooms, a wild vine,
Entwining every thought of mine.

Your specter haunts my waking hours,
A presence felt with ghostly powers.
Like faith that grips a zealot's core,
You've become the god I adore.

If divine hand has played its part,
In forging this connection's start,
Then surely this attraction's might
Is souls reuniting, taking flight.

From time long past to present day,
Two spirits finding their way,
This fatal draw, once feared, now seems
The echo of celestial dreams.

LOVE: AN ASCENSION

To be as Love, a balm for hearts that ache,
A sweetness to dissolve the bitter tear.
This is the path I yearn to undertake,
To bring solace and banish every fear.

My Lord, I plead, bestow upon my soul
The will to persevere upon this road.
Grant strength and purpose to achieve this goal,
To bear with grace this self-appointed load.

For in her name, a universal truth:
L.O.V.E. transcends the bounds of single hearts.
It's not for one alone, but all, forsooth—
A gift divine that healing light imparts.

How many souls have found in your embrace
A sanctuary from their worldly strife?
How many spirits, touched by your sweet grace,
Found strength renewed, a resurrection of life?

Your name itself, a gentle, firm command:
Love freely, and from ailments you'll be freed.
This remedy, so simple, yet so grand,
The truest cure for every human need.

The rung you've reached upon this lofty stair
Uplifts us all, inspires us to rise.
O Love, ascend! Your climb beyond compare
Reveals the path to our own paradise.

WHO WILL YOU LOVE

Time's river flows with glacial pace,
As I stand sentinel on its shore,
Awaiting that transcendent grace—
Your presence, which I so adore.

Each heartbeat marks a moment's flight,
Each breath, a sigh of longing's tune.
I yearn to hold you, day and night,
To feel our souls entwine, in tune.

To see your face, a beacon bright,
To trace your form with trembling hands,
To resurrect our past delight,
And forge anew love's golden bands.

If fate should grant this fervent prayer,
What rapture would my breast unfold!
My heart, an altar warm and fair,
Where passion's flame burns bright and bold.

This fire within, it smolders still,
A spark that waits your gentle breath.
One word from you, and it will fill
Our world with light that conquers death.

But tarry not, my distant star,
For time's cruel march knows no reprieve.
This aching void, stretching so far,
Threatens the very air I breathe.

If longing's knife should pierce too deep,
And silence claim this yearning soul,
Who then would your affections keep?
Whose love would make your spirit whole?

So hasten, love, across the miles,
Let not this flame in vain expire.
For in the warmth of your sweet smiles,
I find the strength to brave time's fire.

Our love, a tale not yet complete,
A song whose final verse awaits.
Until that day our souls can meet,
I'll guard the flame that anticipates.

VOICE OF SELF-DISCOVERY

A WANDERING SOUL

I walked with no direction down the weary street,
Just drifting, observing, as people passed by fleet.

My thoughts turned inward to the world's disarray:
Crime and addiction blurred the light of day.

But what of purpose in this fleeting life?
I pondered my path - whence and whither's strife?

"Find God," a voice replied, "your answer lies therein."
"God?" I questioned, walking on without faith's kin.

A girl alone on the sidewalk caught my gaze,
Her head bowed o'er pages that stole her gaze.

"Why so sad, small one? What disturbs your scene?"
"I scribble words but grasp not what they mean."

Woes beyond number - wars, plague, each land's plight
Children bereft, in darkness' shroudless night.

Helpless I walked, to nothingness consigned -
Til heavenward a call my wandering mind.

"Have hope, pilgrim, though hills and deserts bar -
Look to the stars that guide though dim their spar."

AT THE CROSSROADS

My heart stands at a crossroads torn,
This indecision leaves me forlorn.
To choose 'tween two is no easy task,
Leisure a luxury I must bask.

A cherished place you have in my soul,
Yet another claims a tender role.
My spirit soars to celestial spheres,
Where an immortal love appears.

You are here in this moment with me,
Yet my temple holds a memory.
There refuge he found in joy divine,
Little thought the envy you'd intertwine

WITHIN THE
LOOKING GLASS

Seeking joy's gleam, I chanced 'pon a mirror's eye,
"Wanderer, why flee'st thy visage passing by?"

"What boon's there seeing myself if in soul there cries
A road untrod where bliss' sweet spark lies?"

"Thee shall weary and breathless become on ways long wound,
Thee shall tire and mourn - within these depths thy heart is bound."

"Why plead thee thus, old friend of memories past?
If in myself and heaven's blue I see at last?"

"The track thy soul pursues leads to solace's grove,
Happiness sought without is found alone within, light from above."

A SOUL REDEEMED

Once more I found Don Jesús bowed low by wine's sway,
What pity wrenched my heart at his poor array!

"Speak pray, what word assuage this ache?" he begged, distressed,
"Forgive if e'er I strayed, memory now laid to rest."

"Peace, dear friend, the past's shroud now drawn," said I,
"No rancor sears this breast to thy injury."

Full many sleepless nights and tears fell for past offenses
Harrowing drunken failings neath remorse's senses.

"My days hence walk paths healed; ancient wrongs I forgive."
"Ah blessed chance to lift this soul so sorely riven!"

Now tell Don Chuy, what drove thy will to darkness' den?
How find surcease from Love's loss in vices' ken?

"Since my beloved's gone, for me joy's light is slain."
"Arise, friend, see the sun returns to thee again!"

"Thy life reborn in grace shall teem with mirth anew,
Love first thyself to love and be by others loved true."

"Break bondage' chains and heavenward in freedom fly,
Transformed in soul beneath the sun's bright eye!"

THE ETERNAL'S DREAM

The Lord of Ages numbers no years in His sphere,
For in Timelessness alone does His being appear.

Though fettered to none, His influence wanders free,
Where spirits commune, there dwells His Deity.

No bounds divide man from man in His eyes,
Each soul reflected within His vast size.

One flesh He shares, in each visage His glory seen,
Countless worlds His thoughts shape, lives ever new between.

That Lord dreams none but Himself may view,
In phantasms of Fancy finds solace anew.

Does He, like ourselves, feel, ponder, draw breath?
Inspirations swaying dawn through death?

Within memories' veil retreats my troubled mind,
Anxious no more where Etern waits concealed behind.

This learning my thoughts bring - He numbers no years passed,
For above Time's stream reigns He vast.

DREAMER'S REVELATION

In yesterday's reverie, I schemed
To steal your heart, or so it seemed.
My fingers traced your hands in air,
My gaze caressed your skin so fair.

A canvas of the mind unfurled,
Where you and I, our love-flag furled.
In this sweet madness, I was lost,
My heart aflame, by passion tossed.

I yearned to offer all I own,
My life, my heart, to you alone.
A sacrifice I'd gladly make,
If only your love I could wake.

But lo! Today, dreams take new form,
Reality outshines the norm.
My humble heart can scarce contain
This joy that courses through each vein.

My love for you, a boundless sea,
Grows deeper than it used to be.
To heaven's throne, my prayer ascends:
"Bless this love that never ends."

From fantasy to truth sublime,
Our hearts now beat in perfect time.
What once was dream is now our story,
Love's sweet, unexpected glory.

FINDING MYSELF

In solitude's embrace, I thought I dwelled,
My world a void, crumbling at my feet.
Through meditation's gate, my spirit swelled,
And in that silence, Christ and I did meet.

As contemplation deepened day by day,
Veils of illusion gently fell away.
In God, both Mother's love and Father's might,
I found myself no longer lost in night.

A fragment of the divine, I came to see,
Was housed within this mortal frame of mine.
Self-love, a sacred task, was meant to be
The purpose of this journey so divine.

Through countless lives, this soul has wandered far,
Each body but a temporary car.
Imperfect still, I walk this earthly stage,
A student in life's ever-turning page.

Thrice did death's shadow fall across my path,
Thrice did I rise, my time not yet complete.
For I've a mission, born of cosmic math,
A destiny my soul has yet to meet.

So here I stand, awakened to my role,
A being of light, at last becoming whole

I AM WHO I AM

I stand complete, no fractured half-formed thing,
A being whole, creator of my fate.
Within me, opposites find balance, bring
A harmony that I alone create.

My thoughts are mine, and should I err, I'll bear
The weight of consequence without demur.
To blame another is a snare
That breeds mistakes and makes the vision blur.

This mortal frame, my teacher and my guide,
Has served me well in life's grand learning hall.
Each triumph, stumble, taken in my stride,
For this is why I heeded spirit's call.

When self-awareness dawned, I made a vow
To cherish this corporeal vessel true.
A challenge steep, yet time will show me how
To honor flesh as much as spirit due.

Each moment holds a lesson, small or great,
Though grasping this takes patience, time, and skill.
From world without and realms that lie innate,
I glean the truths that help my soul distill.

This wisdom gained; I'll carry when I part
From earthly bonds to realms beyond the veil.
It's destined thus, though hidden from the heart
Of those who've yet to read life's hidden tale.

Our journey's aim: to learn, to grow, to be
The finest humans we can hope to grow.
And once achieved, we'll set our spirits free
To climb yet higher, to forever know.

Perfection beckons, distant star so bright,
We reach forever, lesson by lesson.
Each day we strive, gain wisdom, seek the light,
Our souls evolving in life's grand procession.

I am who I am - complete, yet ever growing,
A work in progress, finished, yet still flowing.

DARE TO!

What paralyzes you? Is it rejection's specter?
So what if it is? Will it consume your being?
Ah, I see—childhood wounds still raw.
Perhaps a mother's dismissal

Left your heart in tatters.
But listen: you can rise above.
Dare! A 'no' bears no mortal wound;
One door closes, another awaits your knock.

Rejection cannot extinguish your light.
Stand tall, and respect will follow.
So dare to unbind your heart,
Forgive those who've carved their scars,

And let love burst forth unrestrained!
Cast aside the cloak of anger.
Banish the bitter dregs;
Step from the shadows into the fray.

Dare to live!
Your circumstances don't define you.
Embrace love with arms wide open,
Welcome it like a long-lost friend!

I AM A FREE SPIRIT

Unbound, I roam the world,
Unburdened by the ancient shackles
That weigh upon humanity.

Tell me, kindred soul, what does freedom mean to you?
Do you find comfort in your constraints?
I am a free spirit!

As I journey, I hear the lamentations of countless souls,
And I wonder: why can't they see
That awakening is within their grasp?

Observe the slumbering masses,
Blind and deaf to the reality beyond their confines.

They bear the weight of chains
Forged centuries ago,
Passed down through generations,
A legacy of limitation.

So I leave you this message, my kindred soul:
Let your spirit soar in pursuit of liberation.

For I am a free spirit,
And you can be one too.

LEARNING

Our presents intertwine, yet stand apart—
Yours anchored now, mine drifting to and fro.
My genesis, a distant counterpart,
Shapes thoughts that from a different wellspring flow.

In life's grand dance, souls enter, exit, spin,
Some linger, rapt by lessons yet unlearned.
While others, wisdom-rich, transcend chagrin,
Ascending rungs their diligence has earned.

But multitudes remain in shackles bound,
Their vanity a weight, a blinding shroud.
In pursuit of joy, they circle round,
Destroying self and other, blind and proud.

O Vanity! Your cruel and sightless reign
Keeps souls from growth, trapped in a loop of pain.

Yet some break free, their spirits learn to soar,
Each lesson etched in time's eternal score.

MY STRENGTH

To night and day, my words I freely give,
But not to those who seek my joy to steal.
Why from the shadows do you emerge to live
By darkening my path, my spirit to congeal?

Lucifer's agent, sent to bar my way,
To thwart the destiny that I must claim.
Yet God, my guardian, will not let me stray;
A guiding star He sends, my course to aim.

This light divine illuminate my road,
Keeping me steadfast by my Maker's side.
Though cross-like burdens increase my load,
My faith, unshaken, shall in Him abide.

Through darkness deep and trials hard to bear,
My strength endures, for God is ever there.

VOICE OF WISDOM

WISDOM IN THE TWILIGHT

Uncle Juan, in your life's waning light,
Can you unveil the secret of delight?

Guide me on which path I should tread,
What actions to take, what words to be said?

Should I embrace the thorns like the rose?
Lavish caresses or stand in repose?

Uncle Juan, I implore, answer true,
Today, more than ever, I turn to you.

Hush now, dear child, and listen well
To the wisdom this old man will tell.

From birth, you carry joy within,
Though at times it's hard to win.

"But Uncle, I suffer!" I exclaim with might.
Yes, child, suffering is part of life's light.

Not all days will bring pure pleasure,
For in pain, we find growth to treasure.

"It's unfair! I'm just a girl, why must I bear?"
Because life decrees it, this we must share.

Remember always, when one path ends,
Another opens, as your journey extends.

"What more can you teach me, Uncle dear?"
Just this: in joy and sorrow, persevere.

Happiness isn't a distant shore,
It's the journey itself, and so much more.

Uncle Juan, your words ring clear and true,
A beacon of light to guide me through.

In life's tapestry of joy and strife,
I'll cherish each thread that weaves my life.

MOTHERLY COUNSEL

My son, if in your youth I caused you harm,
A mother still half-grown and lacking charm.

No tutelage exists for Motherhood,
Its ways by living learnt, though paid with blood.

And so I bid you now, all wrath disarm,
Forgive your mother's failings, spare her balm.

Bear grudges not, they only wound the more,
Steal peace, and shed a mother's soul like gore.

Though lacking love herself how best to serve,
Still for you she cared, in mercy preserve.

No longer condemn, but pity and adore,
With filial love requite the debt you owe.

Make pardon's gift this mother to restore,
And her past errors now with grace deplore.

WISDOM IN WHISPERS

They say life's stream flows ever on without fail,
That growth stems change, the soul starved without love's grail.

Faithless feet tread paths of death in life still trod,
Heart wingless wanders where its shepherd God.

Grant me share of thine fond care, thy bosom's flowers,
Imbued thus I'd drink love's sun forever ours.

With thy heart's fragment I would worlds subdue
For thy sweet sake and live life's days in thrall to you.

Lend me understanding's grain to cultivate compassion,
And tender aid bestows in life's travailed fashion.

None count flawed, none virtuous, so say trusted friends,
Truths bent by perspective as Time's river wends.

WELL-WORN COMPANIONS

My oldest companions I hold most dear,
Through seasons trod they know each road, each mead.

Though torn, though wearied, within and without,
They sheath my feet as none else new may tout.

Not ornament but comfort is their call,
Through them fond steps recall each land, field and hall.

Paths without end their soles recall to mind,
Through them joys, sorrows intertwined I find.

Ask what boon may I grant in parting hour?
Their wish I'll heed to honor service's dower.

"Let us return whence all things wend their way,
Back to the deeps let dust to dust decay."

Farewell, stout friends of journeys long since past,
Your lives have left their marks that shall long last.

THE SOUL'S GUIDING STAR

What now, my soul, in what fields cast thy seed?
What harvests await life's toils, grief's bitter weed?

After such trials by fire, what lessons remain
While Urantia heals and a new cycle's strain?

Have my questionings stirred answer in any breast?
Unfathomed the truths in each heart's depth invested?

Suffering's school, have its teachings made way
For unity's dawn to light sorrow's long day?

Should Sol veil to set on a world reborn,
From whence comes the spark to rekindle thy morn?

Will that change hope awaits be granted mankind -
Transcending old limits, new potentials to find?

Learn empathy's call, see each sister and brother,
Forgiving and healed walk in peace side by side each other?

Mark where Destiny leads, beyond discord's sad stains -
In each who support find thyself, find thy gains?

Face doubts and see truths standing witness within -
Eternal the flicker time masks, fates begin.

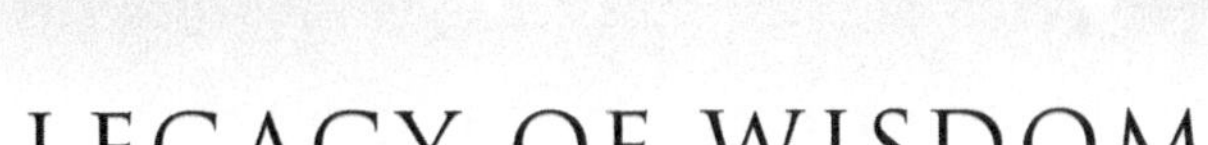

LEGACY OF WISDOM

When I depart this mortal realm, my child,
A treasure trove to you I'll leave behind.
Not coffers filled with fleeting wealth,
But riches of a far more precious kind.

The wealth of knowledge, hard-earned and true,
Shall be your lasting legacy from me.
Guard it well, and watch it multiply,
Beyond what earthly riches guarantee.

This inheritance, unlike mere gold,
Grows richer still when freely shared.
Spread wide the seeds of wisdom gained,
And reap rewards beyond compare.

For in the soil of noble deeds,
The fruits of your labor shall increase.
Not counted in coins or bills,
But measured by lives you touch and peace.

Remember, child, as you journey on,
That true wealth lies not in what's spent,
But in the wisdom that guides your path,
And the love and light your actions have lent.

THE HEALER'S PRESCRIPTION

A sorrow nested deep within my heart,
Its sting as sharp as lemon on the tongue.
This citrus draught, familiar from the start,
Left soul and spirit both by acid stung.

This bitterness had seeped through every pore,
My visage robbed of joy's illumination.
No trace remained of smiles I'd worn before,
My being hostage to this desolation.

Haste, weary soul, to Doctor Isabel!
What balm has she for your corrosive plight?
What remedy to break this acrid spell
And coax your dormant gladness back to light?

Her loving gaze, a salve upon my pain,
Prescribes with wisdom born of gentle care:
"Let smiles, abundant, be your first refrain,
A shield against the sourness you bear."

"Cast off your worries," comes her next decree,
"For they but feed the acid of your woe."
Heed well this counsel, and you'll surely see
Miracles bloom where bitterness did grow.

A SPIRITUAL GUIDE'S EMBRACE

Beneath Hope's shade each soul finds sheltering rest
Through trials unseen an aid brings solace blest

O watchful Friend who calms life's turbulent sea
By your sure hand all enemies conquered be

Lead onward this pilgrim heart with vision clear
Along destiny's path lay no shadows of fear

Lest doubt or fear steal the soul away
Keep watch, I pray, on each winding way

Be near in joy, in sorrow my comfort true
Your guiding light life's deepest mysteries construe

Within your care each spirit finds its worth
And blessings count to serve in Love on earth

A GUIDING DREAM

Within dreams' veil, your presence came
And softly spoke my soul's true name

Attentive heart heard wisdom flow
For life's fair wind, for ebb's calm show

Each word retained, each task embraced
By vision's light the spirit graced

Now when repose lifts veils between
Your nurturing visit comes serene

And in soul's field shows future's bloom
Through dreams we converse beyond earth's room

Your blessings shower each wakening hour
While in slumber's realm afresh we flower

VOICE OF LIGHT AND HOPE

HERALDS OF THE LIGHT

Though stalking thorns may pierce these weary feet,
Or pains torment this pilgrim's soul complete,

Still to the world anew my call prolongs -
To share love's lessons in celestial songs:

That we are one great soul in bodies torn,
Divided yet in spirit still reborn;

To lend strong hands where need cries out the most,
Walk hope and faith along the darkest coast;

Face trials with stout heart and temper tests,
Renewal find in dying to self's unrests;

Learn life's eternal rhythms, its ebb and flow,
Awake each morn love's heralds to bestow

THE SPIRAL PATH TO LIGHT

Follow where the spiraling way may lead thee,
Fear not the subterranean trials ahead ye.

Though shadows shroud, thy footsteps sure and tall,
Beyond night's vale waits solace for thee all.

Floating free thy form in light's pure sea,
Soul finds peace, gladness and good liberty.

Eyes unseeing, ethereal manna yields,
Freedom fills thy frame in aureate fields.

Thine inmost core claims communion's start,
Trusting visions of union with the heart.

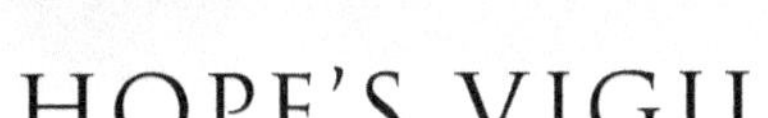

HOPE'S VIGIL

O when shall dawn that bright beatific day
When humankind's countenance reveals thy ray?

When in each face no more indignant guile,
Nor anguish mars sweet fellowship's soft smile?

When hatred turned to love for God above,
And souls on earth find beauty, wisdom, love?

When shall earth's children harvest life's full grain?
When tyranny bow to veridical reign?

O when shall prudence guide our reasoning powers?
O who shall emancipate man's weary hours,

That hand in hand as siblings we make pace
To that fair realm of truth, and peace, and grace?

Still let Hope keep unslumbering watch, her lamp aglow
Till morning breaks on hearts made pure as mountain snow.

DAWN'S EMBRACE

Awaken me with tender kiss,
Your touch, a gentle morning bliss.
Let fingers trace a sensuous trail,
As dawn's arrival we curtail.

Two hearts, one soul, our bodies twined,
By fate's design, our lives aligned.
The rising sun, our love's cocoon,
Two melting hearts, a lover's boon.

As golden rays caress our skin,
I'll whisper truths that dwell within:
"My love, this day, I've given all,
My heart responds to your soul's call."

My essence, yours, a sacred gift,
This moment's joy, our spirits lift.
Your love, a blessing pure and bright,
Illuminates my day and night.

When twilight paints the sky anew,
Our passion we shall yet renew.
In night's embrace, our hearts entwine,
Eternal love, yours and mine.

Each dawn and dusk, a promise kept,
Of love profound, of vows unwept.
In light or dark, our bond holds true,
Forever me, forever you.

DAWN'S SUPPLICATION

As dawn's first light paints hope across the sky,
A thousand heartfelt prayers to You I send.
Not for myself alone, these words I cry,
But that, like sunrise, I too might ascend.

Grant me, O Lord, the grace to see that day
When Earth renewed casts off its tarnished guise.
Let me behold humanity's true way,
Stripped of the veils of vanity's disguise.

Illuminate, dear Father, clouded minds,
That actions spring from hearts both pure and true.
If shadows of malevolence one finds,
Let but one ray of Your light pierce them through.

In You I trust, this darkness shall not last,
Though patience we must find as seasons turn.
In Your own time, this trial will be past,
And in that dawn, Your wisdom we will learn.

A NEW DAWN'S SONG

In solitude's shade once dim hopes lay
Till your light showed soul its lost way

As blood once chilled now thrums warm within
Your presence lifts where gloom had kept grim

Your gentle grace has wrought renewing change
Once bare fields held promise new to range

Feelings fragile stir life's deep wells
As timid love its first bud unfolds

Petal by petal dawn's colors gleam
Within your care found solace's dream

Come bask awhile through joy and woe
This pilgrim soul safe harbor knows

Heart shelter gives to nurture care's seed
In togetherness let hope increase

A SPIRITUAL ASCENT

Within the heart dwell mysteries to heal
As forgiveness' balm makes hurt reveal

Each whisper soft, an etching on the soul
Carving compassion's path to make it whole

A new self rises from past pain set free
Destined for peace, a bright dawn to see

All souls who crossed once bearing dark's sting
Are held now in light and understanding

Turning the cheek shows strength, not fear's yield
By mercy's wings the spirit onward is borne

Each deed redempt, new heights come into view
Self-mastery found by old wounds seeing through

With memories that nurture not accuse
The bright future calls old shadows to loose

This way, hand in hand, all travelers part
As within one loving spirit made strong each heart

THERE IS ALWAYS
AN OPEN DOOR

Hope's threshold stands forever wide,
For those with will to find a way.
Your dreams, a compass and a guide,
Can lead to brighter days, I say.

In childhood's realm of boundless dreams,
I glimpsed the promise of my goals.
Yet doubt, like shadow, often seems
To dim the light of striving souls.

But hark! An open door awaits!
Beyond the naysayers' refrain,
Your spirit's strength anticipates
The triumphs you've yet to attain.

I gasped for air in seas of doubt,
A fish bereft of native stream.
While others' words, a stifling drought,
Threatened to drown my cherished dream.

Yet where there's will, a path unfolds!
Through thickets dark and deserts vast,
The heart that true ambition holds
Will reach its destination at last.

"Just a child," they'd whisper low,
Their words a cage of disbelief.
But in my heart, I came to know
My aspirations' sweet relief.

If you desire, you can achieve!
Let passion be your guiding star.
In your potential, do believe,
For it will carry you so far.

When dreams are pure and intentions true,
Let no one tarnish your bright goal.
The future's canvas waits for you
To paint the longings of your soul.

This truth I'll shout from every hill,
From rooftops high and valleys low:
An open door awaits you still,
Toward it, bravely, boldly go!

VOICE OF TIME
AND MEMORY

ALL TIMES ENTWINED

Here thoughts entwine betwixt the page once more,
A thousand worries waft from soul's deep store.

Hope this now fades to then in fleetest fashion,
As past recedes more ancestral, fact flows into passion.

Wish morrows prove than present pains less sore,
Than antecedent and yesterdays deplored.

As lives progress, these moments find conjoint,
When thought binds all in recollection's point.

For past and future feed the seeds of now,
Through time's full cycle souls their harvest plow.

THE FADING SUN

In bygone days, by grace divine,
I knew a man of curious design.
A father he, with children many,
Yet one alone he cherished plenty.

His youngest daughter, fair and bright,
Hair spun gold in summer's light.
Whispers dark and rumors spread,
Of motives best left unsaid.

His admiration knew no bound,
In her, perfection he had found.
No other woman could compare
To this young girl, so pure and fair.

But Time, that thief of youth and grace,
Moved on at its relentless pace.
The girl-child grew, her glow subdued,
A woman now, her path renewed.

No longer does she shine so bright,
Her golden aura dimmed from sight.
The eyes that once saw only sun,
Now see a mother, life begun.

With child within and babe without,
She walks a road of joy and doubt.
The man who once saw her divine,
Now watches as their paths untwine.

In this tale of time's cruel sway,
We see how youth can slip away.
Yet in the fading of the light,
New life emerges, just as bright.

NOSTALGIA

Times past inspire reflection's yearning gaze
As memory warms with nostalgic rays

Grandparents' tales told with heart and soul
Verse's rhythm soothed life's journeys long and slow

Those school days stir with poetry's sweet charms
Pages pastoral kept wonder safe from harms

How Felipe walked with word and will
Guillén taught through travelling ways life's truths to fill

Bécquer's rhymes echo soul's mysteries deep
Otero's gifts to Creator now in heaven reap

Espronceda's spirit lifts from dust of years
Sor Juana shares through "Foolish Men" wit and tears

Lorca's vision blooms 'cross Wat'rings vast
A Poet found where visions are cast

Though times change, certain joys remain
Within each heart its songs will always reign

WHEN I WAS A GIRL

In my girlhood, I heard whispers—
Murmurs of love, elusive and strange,
A forbidden word, shrouded in fear,
Like unrequited passion's hidden range.

No dashing lads with bouquets in hand,
But curious boys with letters, discreet.
What sweet nothings did those pages hold?
Carnations sketched 'round hearts, bittersweet?

The contents remain a mystery still,
But custom declared love taboo,
A looming threat, a dangerous thrill,
To be shunned, or so they all knew.

"A sin!" my grandmothers would exclaim.
"But what of feeling it?" I'd ponder.
"Does it make one's teeth ache with shame?"
Their warnings made my heart grow fonder.

"Not teeth, but hearts ache," gossiped one,
Long-eared and sly, with knowing glance.
But why such intrigue, such fuss and run,
When joy's remembered from love's first dance?

Why label it sin? Why try to suppress
A feeling that grows stronger still?
The more it's forbidden, I must confess,
The more it bends to passion's will.

It's minds closed tight with prejudice
That fear love's wild, untamed embrace.
If souls entwined must make sacrifice,
Then let them, with unfettered grace!

For love, once whispered, now I shout,
Is not a sin, but life's sweet song.
Break free from fear, from shame, from doubt,
For in love's arms is where we belong.

THE PLACE WHERE I WAS

In slumber's realm, a vision unfurled,
October's chill permeating the air.
A dreamscape both familiar and strange,
I found myself transported there.

Amidst a queue of patient souls,
Awaiting my turn, order in mind,
A stranger burst upon the scene,
Urgency in his eyes defined.

"We must depart," he whispered low,
His grip on my hand both firm and kind.
Down winding streets we swiftly flew,
Leaving the known world far behind.

"What peril looms?" I dared to ask,
My voice a tremor in the night.
His gaze met mine, a balm of calm,
Amidst the growing, unseen fright.

"Look not behind," he urged me on,
"For death's dark shadow swiftly nears.
Many have fallen to its touch,
Their fates now sealed in silent tears."

A thunderous roar split the air,
Heat licked my heels with fiery tongue.
His words echoed in my mind,
As o'er a fence we swiftly swung.

Temptation whispered, "Turn and see,"
As I cleared the barrier's crest.
But wisdom stayed my curious eyes,
As forward still our path progressed.

When finally I dared to glance,
At the place where I had stood before,
Nothing remained but empty space,
The world I knew was there no more.

In waking's light, I ponder still,
The meaning of this spectral flight.
Was it a glimpse of things to come?
Or fears that haunt the depths of night?

The place where I was exists no more,
Save in the chambers of my mind.
A dream, a warning, or a sign?
The truth, perhaps, I'll never find.

WHEN I WAS TWO
YEARS OLD

At two, I gazed at mother's swollen form,
Confusion etched upon my infant face.
"Is she unwell?" I wondered, quite forlorn,
Her shape unlike others of her race.

Then time unfurled, a newborn filled our home,
My eyes drawn back to mother's shrinking waist.
"In bellies, babies grow," the answer shone,
But deeper questions soon my mind embraced.

How life begins, a puzzle long unsolved,
As years progressed, some answers came to light.
Yet one query persisted, unresolved:
When does the soul with flesh and blood unite?

In dreams, a vision granted me a clue:
A spark of light, from mother's form it flew,
To pierce the babe's soft crown and find its rest,
Nestled deep within the beating breast.

An angel whispered, "Guard this secret well,
The soul's true home, a mystery divine.
For mankind's grasp of life is but a shell,
Their understanding frail as yours and mine.

The vastness of the cosmos, unexplored,
Mirrors the depths of life's enigma still.
To know too much would leave you overawed,
Such knowledge has the power to maim and kill."

So here I stand, a witness to the spark,
A keeper of the truths that dwell in dark.

UNTIL WE MEET AGAIN

Life's tapestry, woven with threads of strife,
A tumultuous journey, day by day.
I search for glory in the fabric of my life,
But memories elude me, faded and gray.

Where have they gone, these fleeting scenes?
These moments of triumph, now out of reach.
I grasp at shadows, at half-remembered dreams,
Like trying to hold water on a beach.

Are they hidden in lives I've lived before?
Echoes of past selves, long since shed?
Or do they lurk behind some future door,
In a present I've yet to understand?

Perhaps they're scattered across time and space,
Written in languages I've yet to learn.
In cosmic ink upon the universe's face,
Waiting for the day of my return.

It matters not where these memories dwell,
Nor in what tongue their stories are told.
For this is the hand that fate has dealt,
A mystery my soul is bound to hold.

So I'll embrace this enigmatic dance,
This quest for self in time's vast sea.
Until we meet again, by cosmic chance,
When lost memories come flooding back to me.

In that moment, past and present align,
And all that was hidden will be clear.
Until then, I'll seek the grand design,
In each new day, in each passing year.

VOICE OF NATURE AND LIFE

THE WITHERED
ROSE'S LAMENT

By the river's edge, a rose once stood,
Petals drooping, stem bent low.
Parched and weary, she softly plead,
"A drop of water, is all I need!"

But you, oh river, rushed swiftly by,
Not a glance spared for her desperate cry.
Your waters flowed, indifferent and cold,
While the rose's fate remained untold.

One dawn you woke, with her on your mind,
Searched high and low, but what did you find?

No trace of the flower that begged for aid,
Her memory like mist beginning to fade.
"Where is the rose that thirsts so?
The one I ignored not long ago?"

You raced along your winding track,
Hoping against hope to bring her back.
But time, alas, waits not for remorse,
And kindness delayed often brings discourse.

For there where the rose once stood so brave,
Now lies naught but a withered grave.
Oh river, remember this tale so grim:
Compassion withheld can life's light dim.

For want of a drop freely given,
A beautiful soul from earth was riven.

THE TENDER SAPLING

Within my garden's soil a sapling green took root,
With hopeful care its early growth I did salute.

But soon its leaves grew wilted, branches limp and sere,
What blight, I wondered, caused such woe and fell to fear?

What property possessed that grasping palm, I asked,
That in a night stripped my young hope of sunshine's task?

Was it the chill that killed, that touch so cold within?
Or dearth of care's soft sustenance the fatal sin?

The cause remains veiled still, yet mourn its loss I must,
Lesson of tender nurturance borne on soil now dust.

My solace lies in sowing seeds again with vow,
Through seasons changeless stays sweet Nature's vernal bough.

THE STIRRING TIDE

"Which tide runs truer, that ebb'd or this present sea?"
To such a question lost, my answer wandering be.

Yet a surge sense, assault on norms long held,
Norms once like ramparts stout, now battlements all furl'd.

This tide works change o'er all the land it sweeps,
What was is not, as civic conscience sleeps.

Say not my steps stray from truth's strait way,
A youth not schooled yet in life's trade and sway.

But I'll raise my voice though years be few,
Awake my heart though wisdom trails virtue's righteous cue.

Let inward peace my outward speech direct,
The callow seasons teach before I hope for respect.

ANIMAL BEING

Life transcends mere carnal desire,
At least in my eyes.
If that's your sole pursuit,
Then leave me to my own device.

Passion, a fleeting haze,
Obscuring rational thought.
Not a genuine emotion,
Nor a whisper from the heart.

It stems from the primal self,
Long dormant within your core.
This feral essence now awakened,
Has dimmed your moral light.

Today's world, a reflection
Of this bestial infection,
An epidemic of instinct,
Eroding our human distinction.

MY GARDEN SANCTUARY

In my garden, I find solace, stress melts away,
As plants transport me to a realm serene.
Their verdant whispers soothe my weary soul,
A green embrace, where worries intervene.

Bananas sway, tamarind branches reach,
While mangoes, guavas, moringa stand tall.
The mamey's sweetness perfumes the air,
And coconuts, ever-present, heed my call.

Once, plum and nance and lemon graced this space,
Till nature's fury—a cyclone—swept through.
Yet some blooms remain, defiant and bright,
Painting my world with their resilient hue.
For healing, my garden's a treasure trove:
Lemon balm whispers sleep into my nights,
Maguey's miracle touch dispels ill health,
Aloe vera, "Miss World," soothes and delights.

Kalanchoe, bitter yet full of promise,
Whispered cures for cancer's dread disease.
Mint settles stomachs with aromatic flair,
While rosemary clears minds with gentle ease.

As dawn approaches, I bid fond farewell,
Watering can in hand, a final round.
Before Sol rises to claim the new day,
I leave this sanctuary, joy profound.

In this small Eden, I've found my retreat,
Where nature's rhythms calm life's ceaseless race.
My garden: healer, teacher, and dear friend,
A verdant haven of tranquility and grace.

EARLY RISINGS

As dawn's first rays peer through curtains' veil
A sleepy mind still wishes to sail
On dreams winding, e'er their tendrils part
From slumber's realm where joy fills the heart

But feathered heralds their songs now raise
To greet the new day's awakening rays
Their calls remind life's next chapter's due
sweet rest must end, tasks wait to imbue

Yet the soul still lingers where comfort lies
And bids its friend the sun to surmise
"Let me linger but a breath more, I pray
Till rested strength for day sees me on my way"

Too soon each moment flees on time's quick stream
The newborn morn's light bids farewell to dream
New scenes await just past dawn's doorway
Renewed, arise, and greet what the new day may

VOICE OF FAMILY AND BELONGING

A CHILD'S LOVE

The hour struck nine as with a book I passed the day,
When knocks upon the door called thoughts from page away.

"Enter, good friend, the door stands ever open," said I,
Marking where Fancy's flight had led before his eye.

Drawing near he gave with hands made moist by innocent charm,
Two sweets and greetings tucked 'neath words a balm and balm.

Smiled he with mirthful guile and beauty under veil,
"Joyous be this love day!" so spoke without fail.

Lingering there enchanting mischief lit his glance,
As for my answering words he kept sweet attendance.

Ah, could these eyes but fold him in a fond embrace,
And revel childlike hours in soul's restoring grace.

THE PRICE OF BELONGING

Chance encounter on a nameless street,
A ghost from my past I chanced to meet.
That young man who once stirred my heart,
Now stood before me, life torn apart.

What drew me then? I pondered anew,
As his current state came into view.
A leg in cast, on crutches he leaned,
His former grace forever demeaned.

"An accident," my mind quickly guessed,
A twist of fate that left him distressed.
But truth, when revealed, cut deeper still,
No mishap this, but fruits of ill will.

Malice had shattered more than bone,
In quest for bonds, he stood alone.
He'd sought a family in a ruthless gang,
Where violence echoed, cruelty rang.

The broken leg, a visible sign
Of hidden wounds that intertwine.
Something more lurks beneath the surface,
Unspoken pain, a shadowed purpose.

Irony bitter as gall to taste:
His father's pride, so misplaced.
Who introduced this world of strife,
And called it passage to manhood's life.

Oh, what profound wisdom did he share,
This father who led son to despair?
In seeking to forge a stronger man,
He'd twisted the boy's life's whole plan.

Once he made me sigh with desire,
Now he stands, a cautionary pyre.
Youth's promise breaks on jagged shores,
Where belonging exacts brutal scores.

A MOTHER'S LAMENT

I weave a tale of sorrow in these lines,
A story that my heart still undermines.
Of pain and shame, I hesitate to speak,
Yet silence serves the cruel, not the weak.

A mother's tale, her dignity in shreds,
Abused, humiliated, fear she sheds.
But horror compounds horror in this life:
Violation adds to years of strife.

From each assault, new life unwanted springs,
Not born of love, but darkest sufferings.
A degenerate, a monster in man's guise,
Leaves scars unseen by unconcerned eyes.

Such men, like plagues, infest our mortal sphere,
Their acts a blight that we cannot coheres.
If power were mine to end their wicked reign,
I'd cleanse the earth of their polluting stain.

This tale I tell, though it may bring distress,
To shine a light on those who acquiesce.
For every victim silenced by their fear,
We raise our voices, make their stories clear.

In sharing grief, perhaps we'll find a way
To change the night into a brighter day.
For knowledge breeds the courage to resist,
And healing starts when we refuse to desist.

WE ARE ALL CHILDREN OF THE SAME GOD

As I journey forth, my steps unfold,
Sowing seeds of truth along the way.
May they sprout before my story's told,
Before this mortal coil I must lay.

To the wind, I cast these seeds of light,
Trusting currents swift to bear them far.
To lands unknown, beyond my sight,
Where they may grow like a newborn star.

The soil that cradles each fragile seed,
Its quality beyond my mortal ken.
Good or ill, it matters not indeed,
For God alone knows where and when.

The essence of my sowing is clear:
Your words, O Christ, I scatter wide.
The message You've imparted here,
Is what I spread with loving pride.

You planted love within my breast,
Your presence filled my yearning heart.
In my soul, Your truth found rest,
And gave me this sacred part.

"Bear witness," whispered You to me,
"Let My message reach every shore.
Proclaim it loud, set spirits free:
All are God's children, rich and poor!"

So I'll keep walking, planting still,
These seeds of unity and grace.
May they bloom on every hill,
Uniting all of Adam's race.

For in God's eyes, we're all the same,
Beloved children, one and all.
No matter creed or earthly name,
We're answers to the divine call.

VOICE OF TRUTH AND ILLUSION

THE VEIL OF IGNORANCE

How heavily ignorance shrouds our world,
A veil through which truth lies unfurled.

The doctor, armed with science's might,
Forgets the soul's healing light.
Unaware that in harmony they stand:

Body and spirit, hand in hand.
The philosopher, proud of mind,
Believes all truths he's sure to find.
Yet the cosmos, vast and grand,

Holds mysteries he can't understand.
The lover, in passion's warm embrace,
Expects their joy from another's grace.
Blind to the wellspring deep within,

Where true contentment must begin.
The materialist, by wealth enthralled,
Thinks all life's treasures can be bought.
But as coins slip through grasping hands,

Alone amidst empty riches he stands.
We claim to love a higher power,
Profess our faith hour after hour.
Yet wound our brothers with careless deeds,

Ignorant of love's most basic creeds.
O ignorance, that stubborn foe,
How you persist and ever grow!
In hearts and minds you build your wall,

Until we heed wisdom's clarion call.
To shed this veil, we must aspire
To knowledge true and vision higher.
For only when we seek to learn,
Can ignorance's tide we turn.

UNSPOKEN TRUTHS

How heavy the burden of unspoken words,
That should flow freely, yet remain unsaid.
Your mind, closed off, refuses to be stirred,
A truth I've witnessed time and time again.

When reason fails to guide one's thoughts and deeds,
All else falls short, a house built on sand.
I know my words would plant resentment's seeds,
Fury blooming from truths you can't withstand.

Your self-regard, a blinding, brilliant light,
Obscures the flaws you're unwilling to see.
Add spirits to this mix of day and night,
And watch the chaos that's sure to be.

It's not from fear I hold my tongue at bay,
But from a well of patience, hard-won, deep.
Common sense guides me through each trying day,
This wisdom, like a treasure, I will keep.

I see the loneliness that haunts your soul,
A void you struggle vainly to ignore.
But understand: I'm not yours to control,
Nor will I change to settle your inner war.

HOLLOW DECLARATIONS

When "I love you" falls from careless lips,
How can I trust such thoughtless devotion?
Your actions and words are ships that pass,
Sailing different seas, opposing motion.

You weave deceit with every breath,
Aiming to capture my unwary heart.
You place yourself upon a pedestal,
A self-made idol, false from the start.

What folly drives you, what vain hope,
To think I'd miss the subtext of your game?
Your fleeting fancy, a moment's whim,
Reveals itself—how poor your aim!

I glimpse the future, should I yield
To empty words that promise pleasure:
A harvest of anxiety and regret,
Disappointment in equal measure.

Better to part ways, to bid farewell,
Than dance to your discordant tune.
For hollow words, however sweet,
Ring false beneath the fickle moon.

WHERE IS THE TRUTH

A child's questions stir wisdoms seed to root
As grandfather guides their search for Truth's sweet fruit

"Which truth I seek, dear Papa, tell!" cried the young
"In earth below? Or Heaven's heights among?"

With care and patience came the elder's word
"Each place, each moment holds some gleam of Truth inferred

Not just in books or skies its lessons lay
But within life's full flow from dawn to day

When mind and heart inquire with love's clear light
Through patience, empathy, Truth's veils lift bright

No single answer will one place reveal
Its layers unfold as within yourself you feel

With years comes gaining what youth seeks to know
By learning from all deeds and souls you meet life's flowing show

Now rest, my joy, let wonders come in turn
With open soul and time, Truth's ways you'll learn"

LIFE'S GRAND ILLUSION

I've come to see that life,
Is but a shimmering mirage.
A truth etched deep within my heart,
A wisdom hard-won, bittersweet.

This world's a stage, they say,
And we, mere players in the fray.
To reach the zenith of success,
One must outshine the rest.

In this vast theater of existence,
The role I've been assigned
Has touched the core of who I am,
Transformed my very mind.

Now fused—my soul, my thoughts, my pulse,
A singular entity.
How fitting is this part I play,
In life's grand pageantry!

MISREAD SIGNALS

You presume to know my thoughts,
Believe you've read my heart,
Convinced our paths will intertwine
In passion's daring art.

Oh friend, how far you've strayed
From truth's illuminating light!
Our natures, though complementary,
Are day compared to night.

Your allure, I'll not deny,
Is potent as a hive's sweet song.
But think not that I'll succumb
To honeyed charms, however strong.

For if I taste that cloying nectar,
Where then shall I find relief?
I'd rather keep my tranquil stream
Than risk a raging rapid's grief.

Why trade serenity's embrace
For tumult's wild, uncertain ride?
A torrent's thrill may tempt the bold,
But wisdom bids me step aside.

Forgive my candor, if you will,
As harsh as truth can be.
Accept the gift of friendship's bond,
For that's all I can foresee.

VOICE OF INNER STRENGTH

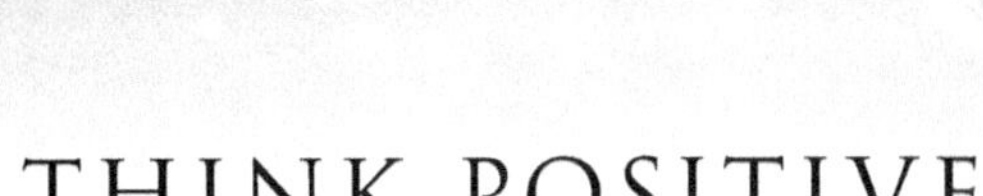

THINK POSITIVE

When life's unfair winds blow your way,
And prejudice casts its shadow long,
Let positivity be your stay,
Banish the negative, stand strong.

Discrimination's tangled roots
Run deep and spread their poison wide,
Its definition coldly mutes
The warmth of human pride inside.

In lexicons of human flaws,
This word might freeze you where you stand,
Its reach defying nature's laws,
Touching every heart and hand.

But let not fear consume your soul,
Nor shatter your inherent worth.
Pity those whose hearts are coal,
Uneducated from their birth.

For they who wield bias as might,
Often bear its scars within,
Projecting outward their own plight,
Perpetuating cycles of sin.

Remember, though, we're not the same,
Each blessed with unique gifts and skills.
Seek the place that fans your flame,
Where your spirit soars and thrills.

Cultivate your talents there,
Let them be your sword and shield.
In a world that seems unfair,
These are the arms you'll wield.

So when you face life's trials anew,
Let wisdom guide each step you take.
Think positive in all you do,
And from old hurts yourself awake.

Our differences, a tapestry,
Woven rich with varied hue.
Embrace your own complexity,
And let your light shine strong and true.

LOVING MYSELF MORE

In night's long embrace, loneliness creeps,
Silence, a paradox, both balm and bane.
Its presence soothes, yet my spirit weeps,
Seeking peace amidst this quiet reign.

Why does this stillness, meant to calm and heal,
Sometimes feel like a dagger to my heart?
Perhaps within its depths, I'll finally feel
The inner peace from which all growth can start.

For in this silence, I may learn to see
The beauty of the self I've long ignored.
As self-love blossoms, setting my heart free,
My capacity for love grows ever more.

And as this love expands beyond my soul,
Touching others with its gentle grace,
I climb the spiritual ladder, reaching goals
That align with Christ's divine embrace.

His mandate echoes through the ages still:
"Love others as yourself," the greatest call.
In loving me, I learn to love until
My heart has room to shelter one and all.

So in this quiet night, I'll sit and grow,
Nurturing the love that starts within.
For only when I let self-hatred go,
Can I truly let God's love begin.

EVERYTHING IS IN
YOUR MIND

"All lies within your mind," the teacher said,
When I, a child, brimmed with countless questions.
For in my youth, curiosity led
To queries born of wonder's suggestions.

"How far can human potential extend?"
I asked, hoping not to provoke his ire.
"It's all within," he stressed, "Comprehend:
A well-honed mind can set the world on fire."

"The path to genius starts between your ears,
Abundance flows, and miracles unfold.
But how to start?" I pressed, all eyes and ears,
"Seek knowledge first," his wisdom pure as gold.

"Must I devour books? Attend grand schools?
I'll knock on every door of learning's halls,
Cross borders, study ceaselessly – no rules
Too strict, no challenge that my spirit stalls!"

He smiled, "Such thirst will carry you afar.
Learn deeply, child, and plenty you shall reap.
Yes, books and schools will guide you like a star,
But know the ether, where all wisdom sleeps."

"There lies the essence of all human thought,
A cosmic library of truths untold.
Immerse yourself, for there, what can't be bought:
The keys to unlock mysteries of old."

So armed with guidance from my sage's words,
I set upon a journey of the mind.
To seek, to learn, to soar like freedom's birds,
And in that flight, my truest self to find.

For in our minds, potential knows no bounds,
When nurtured well, it blooms in wondrous ways.
In books, in schools, in ether's mystic grounds,
Lie seeds of genius waiting for our gaze.

YOUR WORST ENEMY

In life's long journey, I've come to discern
That forgiveness unlocks miraculous gates,
A prison break from where we yearn,
Escaping bonds that bitter heart creates.

Where hatred and resentment long have dwelled,
Corroding spirits in their secret lair,
The unsuspecting soul remains compelled,
Unaware it's trapped in its own snare.

Blind to the bars of their self-made cage,
These prisoners fail to recognize
That in this drama, on life's grand stage,
Their worst foe wears their own disguise.

Within, they nurture wounds so deep,
Then cast reflections of their pain.
The hurt they've sown, they're doomed to reap,
Seeking vengeance, but in vain.

For what does retribution yield?
Does it bring joy or peace of mind?
No, suffering's crop infests this field,
For you and all of humankind.

So heed these words, my sister, brother,
Born of wisdom, hard-earned and true:
Cease this war against each other,
Start with the enemy inside of you.

Embrace forgiveness, let it heal,
The scars that time cannot erase.
For in this act, you'll finally feel
The freedom of a higher grace.

I LEARNED THE LESSON

A whispered 'yes' escaped my lips, betraying
The thunderous 'no' that echoed in my mind.
Confusion gripped my heart, its rhythm swaying,
As mortal eyes to higher truths were blind.

My guardian angel, seeing past illusion,
Sought to guide me with a gentle hand.
But human ego, wrapped in its delusion,
Refused the wisdom I'd misunderstand.

Pride's bitter fruit I tasted, day by day,
Disconnected, stumbling down life's hill.
Yet in this bond, a lesson held its sway,
A cosmic classroom, bending to God's will.

Time stretched, elastic, as the test wore on,
A year, then more, in learning's labyrinth lost.
I felt ensnared, my freedom seemingly gone,
By energies that exacted heavy cost.

But Love Divine illumined darkened thought,
A saint appeared to ease my burdened soul.
At last, I grasped the lesson life had taught,
Patience bloomed, making broken spirit whole.

Now, tempered by this journey's arduous length,
I walk with grace where once I would have railed.
In every step, I demonstrate new strength,
A testament to how God's love prevailed.

The 'yes' that once seemed wrong now proves divine,
A doorway to the growth that made me shine.

GIVING IS HOW
YOU RECEIVE

"Open your heart, for giving leads to gain,"
A wisdom oft-repeated, seldom heard.
But in these words, a truth does yet remain,
A cosmic law, in simplest terms conferred.

To reap, one first must sow - this much is clear,
The universe has coded this decree.
Can barren fields yield harvest year to year?
Can empty hands grasp bounty flowing free?

Gaze in the mirror, then your brother's face,
Seek out abundance where it may reside.
In helping others, find your rightful place,
For life's great wheel does ever turn and glide.

A need observed, a chance to lend your aid -
Remember this when fortune's smile has strayed.
For if tomorrow finds you wanting more,
How will you call on what you've not given before?

The law of karma weaves its subtle thread,
Through every act of kindness, large or small.
So give with open heart, free from all dread,
For in your giving, you receive your all.

VOICE OF CHANGE AND GROWTH

THE AUDACITY OF CHANGE

What a turning point
to have dared to run
as a formidable candidate
and shatter the glass ceiling.

A history of power
had been etched in stone,
with golden letters,
and unspoken traditions.

As the world evolves,
so too does our story,
now written boldly
in the ink of progress.

How blind is prejudice,
the mind that fears change,
clinging to the familiar,
resisting the inevitable tide.

And here we witness,
a pioneer stepping forward,
not seeking glory,
but answering history's call.

May your era be blessed,
though fraught with challenges,
stand tall against the headwinds,
for your legacy will endure.

CROSSROADS

Beyond the veil of consciousness,
I drifted to a distant realm,
A place both strange and timeless.

At a nexus where four paths converge,
I found myself amidst a bustling bazaar,
Camels swaying, their bells a gentle dirge.

Moments passed in this alien scene,
When panic erupted, a crescendo of fear,
Voices rising, a terrified keen.

"They come! They come!" The cry resounds,
Merchants flee, abandoning wares,
Tugging camels from their grounds.

Alone I stand, lost and unsure,
As cannons roar their deadly song,
A cacophony I cannot endure.

Suddenly, pain lances through my chest,
A phantom wound from worlds away,
My spectral journey put to the test.

Wrenched from my trance, I lie inert,
Weakness seeps through every pore,
My appetite and strength desert.

Agony grips me, threatening to overwhelm,
My chest aflame, I feel life's tide
Ebbing within this mortal realm.

THUS IT IS DECIDED

In dreams, I saw you and loved with fervor,
Yet awake, before you, I'm struck with fear.
My heart, once bold, now seeks to flee and sever,
For the intensity of feeling draws too near.

Gazing upon you, I melt anew,
Imagining the bliss of your embrace.
Why seek elsewhere what I've found in you?
In your arms, I've discovered my place.

If this passion clouds my senses so,
It must affect you in equal measure.
Our connection, a destined ebb and flow,
Together we'll cherish this newfound treasure.

Come, let us love, for fate has spoken,
Our hearts entwined, this bond unbroken.

A PRAYER FOR UNDERSTANDING

If understanding's balm our hearts could heal,
How much ache and woe avoidance would seal!

To comprehend demands forbearance rare,
With insight nourished raise thy soul's hearts' prayer:

Beseeching blessing's boon to lead life's way,
A surer path light in dusk's dimming day.

That wisdom's shrine thrown wide each mind embrace,
And all as one great family find solace's space.

Entreating kinship's bond unite our race,
In fellowship and care redemption's solace we may trace.

VOICE OF SPIRITUALITY AND EXISTENCE

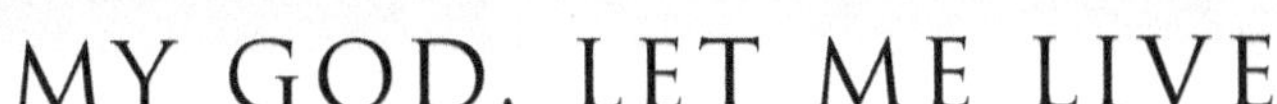

MY GOD, LET ME LIVE

In the stillness of night, upon my bed,
Death's specter loomed, a chilling sight.
Her scythe's cold edge caressed my throat,
A whisper of endings in the pale moonlight.

"For you, I've come," she softly intoned,
Her measured words froze my very core.
Paralyzed, I lay beneath her gaze,
My heart pounding against Death's door.

"Your time has come," she coldly declared,
A statement that shook me to my soul.
"Father above!" I silently cried,
"Is this truly to be my final role?"

"There's so much left for me to learn,
So much of life I've yet to taste.
This world, though flawed, I've grown to love,
Don't let it all go now to waste."

With fervent hope, I prayed aloud,
The Lord's Prayer trembling on my lips.
"My God," I pleaded with all my might,
"Let me live, don't let my light eclipse!"

As if in answer to my plea,
Death's presence began to fade away.
The scythe withdrew, the shadow lifted,
And I was granted one more day.

Now each moment is a precious gift,
A chance to grow, to love, to give.
I'll never forget that fateful night,
When God heard my cry, "Let me live!"

LIVING DYING

In slumber's embrace, a vision unfurled,
Of life ebbing slow, a gradual fade.
Twixt worlds I drifted, neither here nor there,
In twilight realms where destinies are made.

Eons passed in that timeless space,
As consciousness slipped through my fingers.
Awakening at last to a world anew,
Where the echo of that dream still lingers.

While cloaked in sleep, my soul waged war,
A battle between the dark and light.
In that crucible of spectral strife,
I forged resolve for the next life's fight.

"Let this trial temper my spirit," I vowed,
"May each struggle polish my soul."
For in death's shadow, I glimpsed a truth:
That to be broken is to become whole.

I dreamed of dying, a slow descent,
Yet my mortal coil refused to yield.
In that liminal space of half-existence,
Profound mysteries were revealed.

To the cosmic father, I pleaded my case,
"Grant me time," my spirit implored.
"To learn the wisdom hidden in death,
To grasp the rebirth it holds in store."

For in dying, we are born anew,
A phoenix rising from its pyre.
Each ending cradles a fresh beginning,
As night gives way to dawn's first fire.

Now awake, yet forever changed,
I walk the boundary of two realms.
Living and dying, a dance eternal,

Where each step both saves and overwhelms.
In every breath, a little death,
In every death, a chance to live.
This paradox, now etched in my soul,
Is the greatest lesson life can give.

SILENCE

Stillness reigns! The house a sacred space,
Where weary workers seek their earned repose.
In quiet corners, let them find embrace
Of peace that soothes and gently overthrows.

Softly now! A babe in slumber deep,
Lies dreaming in a world of hushed delight.
Let whispers fall and gentle rhythms keep,
As we stand guard o'er sleep's fragile night.

Levelheaded be! When tempers flare,
Eschew the shouts that fracture calm's domain.
No voice raised high can mend the tear,
Compose yourself, let reason's cool remain.

Courtesy calls! For guests have graced our door,
Envelop them in welcome's gentle art.
Disturb them not with clamor's roar,
But let our silent warmth impart.

Elders rest! The grandparents are here,
Deserving reverence in their twilight years.
Tread lightly, speak low, hold them dear,
As wisdom whispers what youth barely hears.

Supper's served! The table set with care,
In harmony we gather, one and all.
Let conversation flow like gentle air,
As we respond to evening's muted call.

Evening falls! The day's last light has fled,
Night beckons all to seek their waiting beds.
Climb the stairs with soft and measured tread,

As silence drapes its peace around our heads.
Each moment holds a call for quiet's grace,
In every line, a lesson to be learned.
Silence shapes the contours of this place,
Where life's most precious gifts are earned.

VOICE OF SOCIETY

VOICE OF THE PEOPLE

I am a voice from the soil, not born to wealth or power,
But with a flame of purpose kindled in my core.
This flame, now a beacon, guides me to my calling:
To uplift my people, to break the chains that bind.

Long have we yearned for true liberation,
Today, we stand at the threshold of change.
I am but a vessel for the people's will,
Tireless in my pursuit of a just nation,

Where the forgotten and the marginalized find their place.
Corruption and violence have cast long shadows,
Staining our land with sorrow and fear.
We cannot—we will not—abide this darkness!

I choose the path of integrity and truth,
Rejecting the trappings of excess,
While others gorge on ill-gotten gains.
Vigilance is my constant companion,

For those who speak truth walk a precarious line.
But I seek not victory through force or intimidation,
My weapons are words, deeds, and unwavering honesty.
This mantle of leadership weighs heavy, it's true,

Yet with faith and resolve, I bear it with pride.
Should I fall in this noble pursuit, I'll rest content,
For in death, my spirit will find immortality.
I'll live on in the hearts of those who dare to dream,

Sparking movements that cannot be quelled.
So I implore you, those who oppose progress:
Step aside, let your bitterness wither and fade.

Allow me to forge ahead, blazing new trails,
Heralding the dawn of a brighter tomorrow.
May this new day shine with hope renewed,
As we, united, build a better future for all!

THE GOOD JUDGE

An old man once imparted
Words of wisdom, indelible,
Etched in my mind forever.
He said, "A nation earns its ruler,

Can't demand more than it gives.
When honor wanes, so does leadership."
Observing life, I've found this true:
Good judgment starts at home,

A lesson we must understand.
Our greatest flaw, a dearth of honesty,
Permeates each corner of our world.
Look closely, you'll see its absence.

Why demand what you can't offer?
Why seek virtue you don't possess?
Before you judge another's faults,
Examine your own conscience first.

Clear your vision, then take action!
When others see your clarity,
They'll follow in your footsteps,
Finding joy along the way.

So, my friend, I urge you:
Embrace integrity!
Plant the seed of truth today,
And reap its fruits tomorrow.

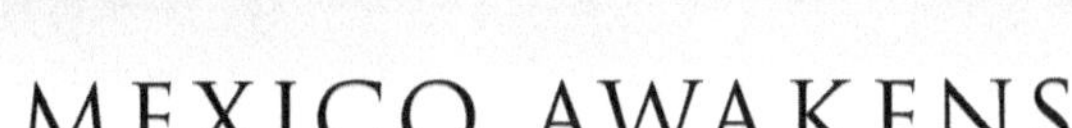

MEXICO AWAKENS

Arise, magnificent Mexico!
Too long have you slumbered.
Your roots run deep, undiminished.

I proclaim your greatness,
To the four winds I cry,
With fervor and pride.

You are Maya, Tarasco, Toltec, Mixtec,
Quiche, Tarahumara, Chichimeca,
Cora, Yaqui, and Aztec!

In this diversity lies your strength!

Your heritage, profound and unyielding,
Allows you, like the phoenix, to rise anew.

Reclaim your legacy in the annals
Of heroic deeds and glory.
Rediscover your lineage
With courage and conviction.

Unite with your people, those who serve
Their brothers and sisters,
Forging a world reborn.

Oh, beautiful Mexico, I stand in reverence,
Echoing Miguel Hidalgo's cry for freedom.

I invoke Morelos, the righteous judge,
Allende, Aldama, and the martyrs
Whose blood consecrated our liberty.

Now awake, I join the chorus of voices.
My skin gleams brown with pride,
For I am Mexico incarnate!

WOLVES AMONG US

Heed this warning, brother mine,
Your eyes must open wide.
For on your path, in fleece so fine,
Fierce wolves in silence glide.

Those showering praise may seem sincere,
Their words a soothing balm.
But daggers wait in shadows near,
To shatter this false calm.

Beware the guise of noble deeds,
A veil for darker arts.
They seek to blind, to plant their seeds
Of doubt in trusting hearts.

In halls of power, truth runs thin,
Rare as desert rain.
Yet those who hold it firm within,
My deep respect obtain.

For they possess a sacred call
To serve with honor bright.
They dream of Mexico standing tall,
Embracing life and light.

But vigilant we still must be
Against wolf-packs disguised.
They'll guard their status ruthlessly,
Leave dreams unrealized.

To live unmarred by corruption's stain,
By crime or hatred's might,
To break impunity's dark chain,
And walk in brotherhood's light.

This is the vision we must hold,
Against deception's art.
With eyes wide open, spirits bold,
We'll give our nation heart.

VOICE OF REFLECTION

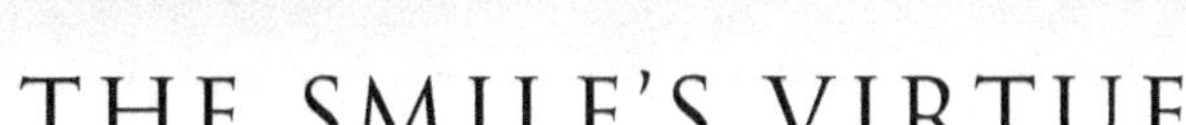

THE SMILE'S VIRTUE

Above all things, cultivate a smile each day,
Its worth in healing learn without delay.

A smile lifts spirits from gloom's deepest well,
Warms the cold heart and cures what ails one's sell.

In good times and ill, 'tis comfort's dearest friend,
When friendship is needed, there to amend.

Priceless gift freely given without fee or tax,
Cherish this ageless comrade, smile's dear knacks!

A smile unlocks closed hearts with caring's key,
Quenches the bitter soul's arid lea.

Through ages past and future, smile stands fast,
By thy side constant in mercy's vast.

With smiling mien each new dawn you may greet,
Happiness drawn to door by smile so sweet.

KINDRED SOULS

Before reflection's glass your human face behold,
See mid surrounding forms birth's primal mold.

As tree your sibling stands, beast lending its mite,
In amity with all find home, life's light.

Nurse first milk's bounty, then sweet Nature's grace,
As offspring nourished both in her embrace.

Sister grass, brother woods, kin zebra roaming wide,
Life's seasons by will breathe not yours to guide.

Born of earth all rise, through cycles wend once more,
One purpose binds - serve brother pilgrim at Nature's door.

Within her verdant halls find solace, learn her lore,
Through reverence know your place mid spheres that spin Heaven's
floor.

Let contemplation seep past language's bounds,
Unite through care and awe 'neath canopy of sounds.

HEARING THE SAME TUNE

A child's heart breaks with each discordant cry
As parents' shouts drown out love's lullaby

"Why must this music play on repeat?
When hugs and smiles I long to greet"

They pledged in joy to build one home, one heart
But now emotions clash and joy falls apart

Wishing the din would fade or find solution
The child seeks solace through reflection:

"What is this love that's so fractured, fear?
I'll learn from this and do better, I swear"

With time and care, hurt hearts may harmony know
But a child's well-being comes before future's vague glow

Wounds heal when anger ends its crusade
New tunes found through listening, empathy, and aid

Perhaps from turmoil good can bud and grow

MONEY IS NOT BAD

"How to attract abundance?"
I asked a friend one day.
His curt reply surprised me,
As he turned his gaze away.

"I shun such thoughts," he said,
"For money breeds only greed.
True wealth lies in the spirit,
Not in material need."

His words, though well-intended,
Stirred a tempest in my mind.
I replied, with careful measure,
Hoping my words would be kind:

"May my query not offend you,
Nor the 'whys' that I implore.
Money itself isn't evil,
It's how we use it, nothing more.

Wielded well, it lifts from squalor,
Misused, it can corrupt the soul.
It's a tool, not good nor evil,
Our intent defines its role."

His anger flared, eyes accusing,
"Look around!" he all but cried.
"See the havoc money wreaks!
Can you still take its side?"

"You're playing with fire," he warned me,
"A creator's words, take heed!
Your reality's distorted,
Blinded by material greed."

I paused, considered his passion,
Then gently pressed my case:
"Where do you see true progress?

In scarcity's embrace?
Where money flows, health follows,
Communities can thrive and grow.
But yes, we must use it wisely,

This truth we both should know.
For money's not the villain,
It's how we choose to wield its might.
Managed well, it vanquishes poverty,
Turning darkness into light."

www.ingramcontent.com/pod-product-compliance
Lightning Source LLC
Chambersburg PA
CBHW020333010826
48970CB00011B/650